SO-ADM-329

WITHDRAWN

JESS KEATING

BUNBUN & BONBON

CAPTAIN BUN & SUPER BONBON

graphix

An Imprint of

SCHOLASTIC

To everyone brave enough
to share their superpowers . . .

Library of Congress Control Number: 2020950063

ISBN 978-1-338-74593-1 (hardcover)
ISBN 978-1-338-74592-4 (paperback)

10 9 8 7 6 5 4 3 2 1   21 22 23 24 25

Printed in China   62
First edition, September 2021
Edited by Jonah Newman
Book design by Phil Falco and Steve Ponzo
Color assistance: Wes Dzioba
Creative Director: Phil Falco
Publisher: David Saylor

CONTENTS

THE PERFECT DAY

It was the
perfect day.

Bunbun and **Bonbon**
were having a picnic.

IT WAS THE PERFECT DAY.

UNTIL . . .

PLiNK!

15

So much for the perfect day.

21

The storm broke the tree and trapped my cape!

We need to move this tree.

But how?! We'd need a great feat of strength!

Feat of strength . . .

Or strength of FEET!

27

. . . in the world!

CRASH

41

44

In the CAVE?!
But it's so dark and
scary in there!

I guess my kite is
gone forever.

47

48

A SUPERHERO PICNIC

JESS KEATING is an award-winning author, cartoonist, zoologist, and creative coach. She is the creator of over a dozen fiction and nonfiction books, including *Eat Your Rocks, Croc!*; *Set Your Alarm, Sloth!*; and the Elements of Genius middle-grade series. She lives in Ontario, Canada, where she's surrounded by books, bunnies, and bonbons. To learn more, tweet her @Jess_Keating or visit jesskeatingbooks.com, where she shares classes and resources for creative living.